minedition

English editions published 2016 by Michael Neugebauer Publishing Ltd., Hong Kong

Retold by Renate Raecke
Illustrations copyright © 2016 Yana Sedova
Translated by Anthea Bell
Rights arranged with "minedition" Rights and Licensing AG, Zurich, Switzerland.

Michael Neugebauer Publishing Ltd.,
Unit 23, 7F, Kowloon Bay Industrial Centre, 15 Wang Hoi Road, Kowloon Bay, Hong Kong.
Phone +852 2807 1711, e-mail: info@minedition.com
This edition was printed in July 2016 at L.Rex Printing Co Ltd.
3/F., Blue Box Factory Building, 25 Hing Wo Street, Tin Wan, Aberdeen, Hong Kong, China
Color separations by Pixelstorm, Vienna.
Library of Congress Cataloging-in-Publication Data available upon request.

ISBN 978-988-8341-27-6

10 9 8 7 6 5 4 3 2 1 First impression

For more information please visit our website: www.minedition.com

E.T.A. Hoffmann

THE NUTCRACKER & the Mouse King

Retold by Renate Raecke

Illustrated by Yana Sedova

Translated by

Anthea Bell

minedition

It was Christmas Eve, and Fritz and Marie, the children of Dr. Stahlbaum and his wife, had been waiting for what seemed like ages outside the door of the sitting room, where the presents were to be given.

"I do wish Godfather Drosselmeier didn't keep us waiting for him so long," sighed Marie. "We can't begin opening presents before he arrives."

Godfather Drosselmeier looked after the grandfather clocks in the Stahlbaums' house, and repaired them when necessary. He was not really a clockmaker, but he was very clever with all mechanical things, and he had already given the children many delightful surprises.

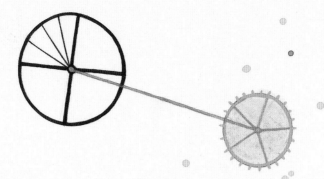

And today he brought them another wonderful surprise: a big, brightly colored box. When the children opened the lid, they saw a stretch of green turf where a sparkling castle stood. The castle had many windows as bright as mirrors, and little gilded turrets. Figures of tiny ladies and gentlemen walked about, or waved from the windows, and then disappeared again.

Fritz and Marie watched, fascinated, but soon they grew bored because once the clockwork people had been wound up, they kept making the same movements again and again. So the pair turned their attention back to the beautifully decorated Christmas tree, where their other presents were waiting.

While Fritz was happily giving orders to a troop of toy soldiers, telling them to fight a battle, Marie saw a little wooden man in the tree, and she liked him at once.

He was really a nutcracker, her father told her. But Fritz snatched him and, by cramming too many nuts into his mouth at once, carelessly broke two of his teeth.

"How can you be so horrid?" asked Marie. "Look what you've done to poor Nutcracker!"

Their father took the Nutcracker away from Fritz and gave him to Marie. "Look after him," he told her, stroking her hair. "He'll be better off with you."

It was late when the children's mother told them to go to bed. Fritz had already put his soldiers away in the glass-fronted cupboard where the children kept their best toys. Marie didn't want to say good night to her Nutcracker yet. "Let me stay with him a little longer," she asked. But her eyes were already closing, and her mother put her to bed, covered her with a warm blanket, and left her to sleep.

Marie was half asleep when she heard the clock strike twelve. Midnight! When the last chime had died away, a whistling and scurrying noise could be heard. Then mice came pushing their way up between the floorboards, more and more mice, tripping and galloping to and fro. Marie lit a candle and went downstairs. What a sight she saw before her eyes!

An owl was perching on the grandfather clock that had just struck twelve, and the owl looked just like Godfather Drosselmeier.
And all the other clocks in the house were ticking and whirring as if in a race against each other.

The troops of mice were drawn up in rank and file in front of the toy cupboard, just as Fritz made his soldiers stand when they went into battle. They were led by the seven-headed Mouse King, whose heads were all hissing and whistling horribly as they turned back and forth, and their eyes flashed in all directions.

Marie saw brave Nutcracker draw his little sword, calling to the tin soldiers to follow him into battle and fight the army of mice.

The noise of the battle was ear-splitting as the fight went first one way, then another. Marie watched anxiously, and when Nutcracker was surrounded on all sides she threw her slipper desperately into the thick of the fray.

At that moment, everything disppeared like a dream, and Marie fell to the floor in a faint.

What's happened, wondered Marie, as she came to her senses;
am I awake or dreaming? She rubbed her eyes. How strange and
different the world around her looked now! Nutcracker had turned
into a handsome young man, and he and she were walking
through the Christmas woods. The landscape was deep
in snow, and a bright star shone from the top of a
lavishly decorated fir tree. Large sugared almonds
lay in the snow, with a mysterious light shining
out of them.

A gateway made of gingerbread, almonds, and raisins, and covered with sugar, opened in front of Marie and Nutcracker, and they went through it.

Candytown, the place they came to, was just what you would imagine a city made of sugar would look like. The streets were made of red and white striped sticks of rock candy. And the sun, moon, and stars were all as sweet as sugar, white and stiff, as if a confectioner had piped them onto the sky with his piping bag.

Marie and Nutcracker got into a boat that was lying beside the bank of the river, like a shell. Colorful flags and banners adorned the masts, and bright sails billowed in the wind.

The boat was drawn by two dolphins, who crossed the great expanse of Rosewater Lake and brought them to an island.

They came to a castle, where four beautiful princesses welcomed them, and told Marie that Nutcracker was a prince, and their brother. But as they went for a ride in the royal coach a silvery mist surrounded them, they could hear a strange singing and whirring in the distance... and Marie seemed to fall from a great height, to land awake in her bed at home.

Had it all been a dream? Had there really been a castle and princesses? She thought she remembered more strange details, but it was hard to know what was real. When she told her mother about how real her adventure with Nutcracker had been, her mother told her it was nothing but a silly dream.

But Marie thought she knew better. And she suspected her clever Godfather Drosselmeier knew that he had given her anything but an ordinary nutcracker. She held it close and thought that the most truly marvelous things may be seen—if only people choose to look.

Afterword

The story of The Nutcracker and the Mouse King, by E.T.A. Hoffmann (1776 – 1822) was first published 200 years ago, in 1816. It is considered one of the earliest fantasies in German literature, for it already blurs the borders between everyday life and an amusing world of dreams and fairy tales.

The story begins on Christmas Eve, when Marie gets the gift of a nutcracker, and her brother Fritz is given a little army of toy soldiers. Marie moves on into dreamland scenes, with wonderful adventures such as the great battle between Nutcracker and the Mouse King.

The ballet based on the Nutcracker story, with music by Tchaikovsky, has been part of the standard repertory of ballet companies large and small for many decades. It is regularly on the Christmas program of many opera houses.

The French writer Alexandre Dumas père, on whose version of the story the ballet is mainly based, followed Hoffmann in part, but he was mainly concerned with providing Tchaikovsky with enough scenes for the ballet, especially in the dances of the second act.

Renate Raecke